MW01130703

# TUMELO

## JERMAINE HUDDLESTON

Copyright © 2021 Jermaine Huddleston
All rights reserved
First Edition

PAGE PUBLISHING, INC.
Conneaut Lake, PA

First originally published by Page Publishing 2021

ISBN 978-1-6624-4042-7 (pbk)
ISBN 978-1-6624-4043-4 (digital)

Printed in the United States of America

Dedicated to you all

# Contents

# Chapter 1

# Stolen Ground

"Tabor, what're we going to do? There've been twenty-two people who've gone missing in four days. Our king is gone, and I imagine we're next. I don't want to get captured, or worse killed by anyone."

"Ada, I don't know. I can't defeat a whole tribe by myself, and I don't know where else we can go."

"Tabor, we have kids, one on the way and an eleven-year-old."

"We don't have many options, dammit! Either we get captured by our own, or we run until we reach a province, Ada."

"Tabor, do you know what'll happen to us if we get captured? We'll be under rule. I don't want our children to suffer. We don't know what they'll make us do, or how harsh they'll be."

"Ada, you're right. As the man of the house, I for once am scared. But tomorrow, I'll make our decision. I am going to bed now. You and Akin should go to sleep as well."

"Fine. I'll go talk to him before we call it a night."

"Akin, my son, are you okay?"

"Mother, I'm scared. What'll happen if we get caught?"

Don't worry about anything, my little warrior. I want you to get some rest."

"But I can't sleep."

"Just close your eyes until you do. Think of good things, and you'll fall asleep. Good night, my son."

"Goodnight, Mother." *I can't just sit here and wait. Maybe my parents can, but I must act instead of rest. My dad is weak, too patient, and I feel as if he wants us to get captured. Maybe I'll rest tonight, but I don't know how long my body will lay.*

"Tabor, wake up. Do you hear that?"

"Go back to bed please. I'm sure it's nothing."

"No, I hear something. Please wake up."

"Fine. I'll go check. Stay here. I'm going to grab my axe just in case someone is here."

"Go check Akin's space first."

*This woman and her damn conscious, I bet there's nothing in here.* "Akin," I whisper quietly. I get no answer, but I clearly see a body underneath the blanket. As I get closer to the blanket, I realize there's rocks underneath. "Ada, he's gone!" Suddenly I hear our straw door open. I rush toward it with my axe. I look outside and see my son running away. I start to chase after him. Once I give chase, I notice a group of three men with torches coming from the woods nearby. They start to chase after my boy. With my axe in my hand, I continue running. We come to a halt, as there is nowhere to run for there is the Atlantic Ocean.

"Please don't hurt my son. We don't have much as a family, but is there something I can do?"

"Your tribe owes us a great debt, plus we know of your wealth, Tabor. Your King has sold all of you out, for his freedom. We have two options for you. You can be under our rule until your debt is paid. Or you can be killed along with the others who tried to resist."

We'll do whatever you ask. Just please don't hurt my family."

"Not I, Father. I refuse to be under any rule. If getting captured is what's ahead of us, I'd rather die a human of great pride. If death is what you wish, then your wish is granted."

"No, please! He's just a kid. Please don't do this. He doesn't understand. Just... I'll do whatever."

"This isn't your choice, Tabor. Don't worry. I'll make sure to make this a quick process for him."

He pulls out a gun, and I rush towards him with my axe. I slice the head off of one of the members, then I'm quickly pushed to the ground with a gun pointed above me.

"Shoot the boy now!" *Bang*!

I scream out to the heavens above as I see my father's body lay limp on the ground. I hear my mother screaming as she runs towards us. Tears running down her cheeks, she grabs my father's head and tells him to wake up. I apologize for running, and all she could do was cry.

"Hey, boy, shut up. Ayo, why'd you shoot the father?"

"Because the boy is young and we could sell him for much more. Now let's start moving. Amare, get the woman. I'll grab the boy. We're headed back to Guinea."

A day has passed. Me and my mother are exhausted and haven't been given any food or water. As the soldiers walk behind us, me and mother look at each other. With my mother being a tough woman, she'd tell me we're going to be okay. We reach a stopping point in our journey, which I'm sure we needed, including the two men.

"Tonight we'll settle here. We'll give you water and food for energy. Here, take these. You and your mother will sleep by that tree. Ayo start a fire, we need to cleanse the water for us. We'll give them sea water for they're undeserving of clean water."

"Mother, I'm sorry."

"Akin, you should've stayed inside. Running away was not a good choice, but I'm not mad. We'll get through this together. We will stay united as a family. Let's eat up, shall we?"

The soldiers give us water along with the nuts and fruits they gave us earlier. Me and my mother gobble up everything and drink the water until there's none left. We lay nestled up against each other until we drift into our sleep.

# Chapter 2

# Captive

I wake up in pain, spitting everywhere and feeling uneasy. I search for my mother. She's nowhere to be found. I look for her while the men are asleep. I hear cries and coughing from the bushes. I go towards that direction. My mother is shaking, and we're both throwing up.

"Akin, we're going to escape," she stated.

"Where to?"

"Son, I don't know but we need to go. The water we drank wasn't clean. It'll only get worse from here."

As we finish throwing up, we're dehydrated and ready to get out of here. As we head in a different direction, we are stopped by a soldier. "I apologize for what we've put you through. I'm just a soldier paying a debt to get my family out of slavery. Take this water and run."

"Thank you so much."

"Go!"

Me and Mother make our way towards nowhere. Only seconds later, we hear a gunshot. *Bang!* The frightening shot sent us into shock mode. We try to jog faster, but my mother is unable to go any longer because of the baby.

"I'm not leaving you, Mother. We're going to make it."

"Akin my son, run."

"He's not running anywhere. You both are going back to our stopping point."

That voice is from the other man, who was asleep. The same one that killed my father. I ran to him with anger. I hit him with one punch. He looks at me with frustration, then knocks me unconscious.

"Akin, wake up. It's time to go, son."

"Mother, what happened?"

"He caught us, that's what happened."

"Get moving. Today we arrive in Guinea. My orders are to take both of you to our king, where you'll be dealt with your consequences. The rest of the way, I don't want to hear a sound from you two. If you try to retaliate against me, you'll end up like that soldier yesterday."

The rest of the way, me and Mother don't say a word. On the way to Guinea, we see villages that are empty. Such an eerie feeling. Gloomy thoughts fill my head. It's been two days since my father has passed, and I'm starting to feel immune. What could be worse than getting captured by someone that looks like you? Of course we're different tribes, but I'm a logical thinker. If we all came together, we could live in peace, and Africa would be a place of love. So many cultures in one place. Too many shepherds and not enough sheep. Everyone wants to be a leader and dictate what they feel is necessary instead of letting everyone have a voice. With my name meaning warrior, it's been ingrained in me that I'm a leader. I can't be too hypocritical of many wanting to be independent with their tribes. While thinking, I noticed my mother has slowed down. Suddenly she breaks down crying and breathing heavy.

"Baby! I… I can't continue."

"Woman, we're almost there. Shut up and walk."

"I have a child in my stomach."

"Lay there then. Reinforcements won't reach you for days."

"Momma, I'm staying with you."

"Says who? She's gonna stay right here. You're coming with me."

I cry as I leave my mother behind. Her screams follow us, but eventually fade out as we get closer to Guinea. As we arrive, I see a mix of different people. I see people everywhere. Most of them were working with animals. I hear various conversations as we walk through crowds. I see people in chains. For the first time, I'm scared. Will this be my life forever?

"Akin's your name, right?"

"Yes, is yours Ayo?"

"Yes. We're going directly to the king where you'll be given your punishment. I'm not sure what he has in mind. Prisoners are here to pay a debt. Some people are sold off for goods. Others are here until the debt is paid off. Whether that's being a slave to us or working with us."

As the soldier tells me about the enslavement here, we arrive at the tribal leader's door. Two guards stand in front of us. Ayo tells them to get Salem. Salem arrives at the door. "King, here's another one."

"Follow me. Are their others or just him?"

"Just him for now."

We enter a room that has a seating area. They start to discuss Ayo's capture of me. He tells Salem that he killed my father, left my mother, and killed the other soldier. He explains everything and then Salem asks for my name. I tell him I'm Akin, a name meaning warrior. He slaps me across the face. I didn't ask you what it meant.

"Be careful, King. This kid packs a punch. Ha-ha. While trying to escape, he hit me. I would've killed him and his mother for trying to escape but I think this little one could be sold for a great amount and the mom is pregnant. Well, anyone that's stupid enough to hit a guard is brave enough to become one."

"Ayo, our main goal is to capture them. Round up some men and go back for her now. Akin, I'll speak with you and your mother about your debt once she arrives. For now you'll be in the wooden shacks with the other slaves. Guards, walk him to the middle-aged shacks." I enter the shack and see people around my age. All eyes are on me. They stand up and circle around me. One person pushes me from behind. Without hesitation, I turn around and punch the first person I see.

A boy yells out, "That's my brother!" then charges at me. I swiftly move out the way, causing him to crash into the wooden crates. Guards quickly rush in and snatch us up before anything else can happen.

"We don't tolerate that mess here. You're all here to pay a debt. We will punish those who do not follow rules." Hours later, an older guy from the shack came up to me and said he respected me for standing up for myself. He even asked if I wanted to join him and some friends for supper. I responded with yes. I couldn't tell what time it was, but I wondered when my mother would return so we could talk to Salem.

# Chapter 3

# Friends and Enemies

Dinner is here now, and I sit with the boy and his friends who invited me to be with them.

"What's your name?"

"My name is Akin, and all of yours?"

The boy who invited me spoke first, "My name is Berko. This is Kahn and Mabel."

"Nice to meet you all." We sat there for the next thirty minutes discussing what's going and their journey here. Mabel states that her village was burned down. Berko and Kahn said their people died while trying to escape. I explained that my father died trying to protect me, and my mother got left on our journey. But the guards are bringing her back. While talking about my situation, Salem approached me and brought me back to his hut. I hear faint cries as I get closer to the designated room. I enter the room and see my mother covered in blood. I run to her side. Ayo stands there with his hands covered in blood.

"Akin, your mother has lost lots of blood and may not make it much longer."

Salem calls to Ayo, "Follow me. We have to talk."

"Salem, I don't think she'll make it another day."

"If she doesn't, it'll be you at fault."

"Could we just kill her?"

"She's pregnant. You need to take her to our tribal caretakers. If you ask me another question like that, you'll be the one to die."

"Sorry. I'll take her at once." Salem and Ayo enter the room. Salem tells me what's going on, then Ayo plus more guards come and take my mother away.

"Akin, it's time to rest. Let me walk you back to the middle-aged hut." Once we arrive, I enter and see everyone getting ready to fall asleep. There's barely any space on the floor, and all the beds are taken. Just as I was about to get upset, Mabel invited me to sleep next to her.

"Rough first day, I see. Get some rest. You know you really couldn't stop snoring last night. Maybe some breakfast will shut you up before we begin our duties."

"Very funny, Mabel. Salem hasn't given me a role yet, so I'll go ask him now." As I begin my walk, I notice the same two guards are standing in front of Salem's door. "Excuse me, may I request to speak with Salem?" Once the message passes through, Salem comes outside and takes me on a quick walk.

"What do you want?"

"I wanted to know my assigned station and where my mother is."

"I'm going to be honest with you and I don't want you to say a word back. Akin, your mother is weak because of her blood loss. With weak people, we usually kill them because they can't pay off their debt. But in this case, I plan on making your mother my concubine. She's attractive, and since she'll be one of them, I'll lower your duties. Maybe you could call me father. Today you'll be out in the field, taking care of the animals."

"I'm going to have to stop you right there. My father is Tabor. You will not take my mother as a concubine. She deserves more than that. My family is good as one. Find yourself someone else." He picks up a whip and slashes me across my left eye, then continuously beats me. He beats me shamelessly, blood running down my face, cuts across my body. I start to feel numb.

15

"You forgot I'm the leader around here. I'll kill you without doubt. Looks like you don't need me to tell you anything about your mother. Because you'll be with the medical team as well. Now get going, Akin."

Bruised and battered, I head towards medical. As I walk through this place, I'm getting stares from guards, workers, and small children. My blood leaks across the dirt, the same dirt that my brothers and sisters walk on. We're at war with each other. Sometimes I think water is thicker than blood. Blood makes you connected, but even a connection fails. While transitioning into deeper thoughts, Mabel and the crew sprint over to me. Berko and Kahn frantically ask what happened. I'm unable to speak. My vision is blurred, and suddenly I pass out.

"Akin, please wake up. Please, my son, fight. Fight!" I wake up on high alert. Chills run down my spine. I'm still very much in pain.

"Mother, I can barely feel my…"

"Shh, Akin. Recover. You don't have to explain anything. I can see better than I can hear. I know one of those guards did this to you and I'm going to get to the bottom of this. You have to learn that your actions always have a response whether it's good or bad."

"Mother, you don't understand. I can explain. Salem wants you to be his concubine along with the others. I told him I wasn't going to allow that. He mentioned that I could maybe one day call him father, and I had no interest. He beat me, as you can see."

"Once I'm healed up, we're going to run away."

"I wish that were true, Mom, but unfortunately we can't run from ourselves. Speaking of healing up, Mother, is the baby here?"

"The baby is here and it looks like you have a brother."

"What's his name?"

"His name is Tumelo."

*Bang!* "Mother, what was that?"

"Stay here, Akin, please."

"No, you're still healing. I'm going to check it out." I take a peek outside, and I see tribal warfare. I see Salem and my crew firing shots in the other direction. I must go help so we don't get taken, but I'm too weak to run. Hidden behind barrels outside of the medical room,

I'm spotted by one of Salem's guards. She threw me a gun, and at that very moment I froze up. I've shot before, but I've never shot a person. But I know this must happen. I shot off a few times, which didn't connect. I really have to hold this gun. I almost broke my wrist. This time, I have a grip on it, staring down my victim. I notice it's a kid that looks my age. A kid in warfare—this isn't how it's supposed to be. I go back in the room with my mother and cry to her. Unaware what's going on, I'm ambushed from a member of the opposition. I'm pushed to the ground, and just as he's about to shoot, Salem tackles him to the floor. The gun is knocked onto the floor. Salem yells to pick it up and shoot. I pick the gun up, then point it at the person who knocked me to the ground. Suddenly I began to think about all the trouble Salem has brought on to me and my tribe. "Salem, my father died because of you. I'm beat because of you." Adrenaline running through my body, I aim directly in between the opposition eyes first, breathe deep, and pull the trigger. *Bang!* My mother began crying loudly. "Salem, it's your turn." I point the gun at him and smile before releasing that bullet. *Bang! Bang* was the sound, but a sound not made by me. I look behind me, and it's Ayo.

"I figured you wouldn't want Salem's blood on your hands." The shooting from outside stops, and other tribal members run into the medical room. They see Salem lying in his own blood.

# Chapter 4

# Jurisdiction

"What's going on here, Ayo?"

"I'm Salem's lead guard. You don't ask me anything. This kid right here killed Salem. I came into this room and saw both bodies on the floor, with Akin holding this weapon. I figured as a tribe we can decide his punishment tonight."

I shout out, "I didn't shoot Salem!"

"You're the only with a gun in here, unless you want to blame it on your mother."

I look at his hands, and I notice he didn't have his gun anymore. By this time, my mother is passed out and I'm stuck alone in this situation.

"Tonight, Akin, you'll be placed in a room by yourself while you await the final decision."

Ayo and his guards take me to a dark room where I reside until nighttime. Hour after hour goes by, and I finally get a knock on my door. I open up the latch on my door, and they give me food and water.

"Akin, there's been a verdict made on your situation. We've decided that you will be beheaded by our guillotine. This will take place tomorrow morning. Have a good night."

I have no more tears left. Lied on, beat on, belittled, I'd rather be dead or freed.

Today's the day. I'm not sure what time it is, but it feels like it's morning. I usually wake up during sunrise. I pace around the room thinking about everything and eventually fall asleep again. Someone knocks on the door, telling me it's time to come out.

"Akin, someone has offered to take your spot. Ayo believes it's best to watch the person who replaced you."

"Who replaced me?"

"No one important. Now let's go."

I leave the dark room and go outside. There's tons of people standing outside all looking at me. I'm taken to the front to watch the guillotine do its job. "Hey, Akin, how's it going?"

"Ayo, please leave me alone."

"I do as I please."

"You lied. You shot Salem. We don't like false news here. If you continue to do so, you'll be punished. Shut up and be grateful that it's not a burden on your shoulders anymore. Attention, turn up front as we begin the beheading of this weak person. No value to us, and honestly, we should've done this earlier. Guards, release the blade now."

I scream out "No! Whose face is covered?"

"Would you like it to be yours, Akin?"

Unable to speak, they release the blade. Slash! The head falls right off. Ayo picks it up, grins, and reveals the face. It's my mother. Infuriated, I scream out and run towards him, but I'm quickly knocked down by a guard.

"Akin, you tried to strike me again? I think that's your second strike. It's time we freed you. Today the Europeans come and you'll be gone with the waves. Guards, take him away."

Hours later, I'm brought out to the water with twenty others. I'm amazed. I've never seen a ship. That feeling is short-lived. I'm still very upset and enraged by what happened earlier. Seeing both parents murdered and leaving my brother is killing me mentally and physically. I want to die. Me being taken away by others is something I'm scared of. Ten men abandon the ship and approach us with boxes. Their skin is white, which I've never seen before. My parents never mentioned another color besides brown. I feel nervous as they stand with a certain aura.

Ayo tells them, "We have twenty-one slaves ready to go, but I must see some trade options."

"You know we have exactly what you want. Now give us what we came for."

"No, you must open these boxes."

"You open these boxes yourself."

Ayo opens the boxes and discovers guns and ammunition. "Thanks for being true to your word. We'll need these against other tribes."

"Get out of my face and go back to your master, Salem. Leave me be with these slaves. Get on the ship, I'll explain what's going on." They took us to a cramped room which had little space. "So you've all been traded, as you know. We need slaves like you to grow sugar-cane, tobacco, and cotton in the new colony. We feed you when we want, and any back talk will result in murder or a near-death beating. Hopefully you emptied your body before boarding, because we have a long journey to the new world."

*Chapter 5*

# Lone Wolf

"Tumelo, what's up, man? How're you doing?"

"I'm doing well. Just working in the field like usual."

"You've never caused a problem here. You know we can get you a position working as a guard before your debt is paid. It's better than working in the field with the others. I know Ayo isn't high on you but I can convince him to consider you a spot."

"I'll think about it and let you know if I'm interested soon."

"Kahn, did you overhear that?"

"Yes, I think it's time we tell him what happened to his family, Berko."

"It's been fifteen years. I feel like we should've told him earlier, Kahn."

"Well, how would you tell someone this young what happened? We both don't want him to end up like Akin and suffer. It's only right we tell him before he joins the same people who killed his family. Hey, Tumelo, get over here and help me pick this crap up. Not sure if I should go over to a complete stranger, but it seems important."

"Hello, do I know you?"

"Nope, but we know you. Now listen, tonight I want you to sit with us two for dinner. This is regarding your family, so I expect to see you tonight."

"Wait, you know my family?"

"Yes, I do. Now get back to work before we get punished!"

Nighttime has come, and before I find the person who spoke with me earlier, I make my bowl full of food. While going to get that, I feel a tap on my shoulder. "Tumelo, I didn't introduce myself and my friend earlier. I'm Kahn, and my friend is Berko. Come sit with us." I follow his lead, and we sit in the center of everyone so we aren't by the edge, where the guards are.

"How'd you guys know my name?"

"We've known your name since your birth."

"You'll have to explain everything to me. I know why I'm here. My tribe owes Ayo and his men labor. I was told one of these guards was my father and my mother died from a disease. That's all I know; I'm not sure what my mission in life is, but I feel that being here isn't too bad."

"Tumelo, you're blinded by their former actions. Trust me, this place isn't where you want to be. Me and Berko are the closest you'll have to family."

"Why are you two here?"

"We've been here for a very long time, Melo. We would've been out if we didn't fight the guards after they shipped your brother away."

"My brother?"

"Yes, you have a brother."

"Where is he?"

"I'm not sure, but I'd guess deceased. I'm going to tell you every-thing before you make a decision on being a guard. This is going to be rough. Promise me you'll keep this between us and not let your anger out."

"I promise you. Now tell me. Please, Berko."

Shattered into pieces, I'm unable to move and speak. My life has been covered up in order to keep me sane. I bet the reason Ayo hates me is because of Akin.

"Honestly, your brother possesses a leadership mentality. He wasn't afraid to speak his mind. If he's still out there I'm sure he's in charge. Enough of him. How're you, Tumelo?"

"I want to kill Ayo and every guard that knows my family's story but failed to tell me. I've been lied to for fifteen years. I'm upset. I tell you this. I'm going to become a guard and kill Ayo. I won't act out. I'll continue to do work and play it cool until I have a plan."

"Well, we're not going to stop you. Continue your plan and execute it."

"Sounds good. Have a great night. I'll see the both of you tomorrow."

Looking at life a little different now, I began to stay reserved. I can only imagine that those two weren't the only two who knew my story. As I head to the field to begin work, I'm stopped by Ayo. "Hey, Tumelo, I'd like to say I love how hard you've been working. Me and the guards had a brief conversation about you, and would like to intend a guard position to you. How do you feel about this?"

"Ayo, I would love to join."

"You begin tomorrow. Find a guard and tell him to bring you to me."

"Sounds amazing. Thank you, Ayo." I go over to the field and notify Berko and Kahn what happened. "Guys, please have my back if anything happens. After I kill Ayo, we'll be going away from this place but I'll need time and resources."

"Melo, you got it. Please be safe. We're your brothers. We got your back."

"Thank you. I'll see you both tonight for our last dinner together." While working in the field, I'm approached by the same guard from yesterday.

"Tumelo, I spoke to Ayo for you and he seemed interested."

"He actually came up to me this morning and granted me the opportunity, and I took it! I start tomorrow. Do you mind taking me to see him tomorrow?"

"Not at all. By the way, my name is J."

"Sounds good. I'll see you tomorrow morning."

I'm up bright and early. Today is the day that starts my journey. I've been thinking about Akin, and I wonder if he's still out there. I step outside to view the sky and inhale the fresh air. I grab a bite to eat, then I go search for J. I eventually found him in the field. "Good morning, J. Could you please take me to see Ayo?"

"Sure thing. Are you ready for this?"

"Yes, let's go." We approach the huge hut with guards standing in front.

"This is our newest guard. Allow us through." They slide, and we glide through the entrance. Ayo is seated at his table.

"Tumelo, my son, nice of you to show up. Now let's go over some things. Thank you, J. Excuse yourself. I want to let you know this job isn't as hard as it looks. Ha-ha. You keep everyone in check and go to war until your debt is paid. When your debt is paid, you may leave or stay. Son, listen to me. If you do that, you'll be fine. Do you have any questions for me, Tumelo?"

"Yes. If I decide to leave, will I get to meet my parents? I heard multiple things, but do you have any clue where they are?"

"I'm sorry to tell you this, but as the leader, I want to be as honest as I can. While transitioning to Guinea, both of your parents caught a severe disease that caused them to die. You know I'll always be here for you, Melo. Today you'll train to become a warrior and carry on our brute mentality!"

Days turned into weeks. Weeks turned into months. Becoming a deadly assassin was my only motivation. A bright red heart turned black and cold. I saw a side of myself that I never knew. Protecting others and getting out of this place struck me multiple times. What kind of person would I be to only release Berko and Kahn? But I've become increasingly selfish to achieve a personal desire than to put my energy elsewhere. This journey became richer by the second. Killing the guards one by one would be too noticeable especially if it were the ones I worked daily with. Ayo is the target, and tomorrow's the day. Before going to sleep that night, I sent both of my brothers a note explaining that they should run after shots have rung out during sunset and wait for me in the woods nearby. As tomorrow nears, I feel the pain that Ayo has put my family through. Streams run down my face until I'm in a deep sleep.

## Chapter 6

# Reversed

Today marks the day. The day I get revenge. The day my family watches me slaughter this dictator. Before arriving at my post, I grab some breakfast in hopes of finding Berko and Kahn. I see both men talking with a guard. As I approach them, both parties turn silent. "How's it going, men?"

"It's going well. Just going over today's duties."

"That's odd. Duties are always the same depending on the day."

"Well, you know, just chatting it up man." All three men get up and leave for a different area. Seems unusual. Guards don't really talk or sit with captives. Even weirder, they moved to a different area to get away from me. Before walking to my post, I look at the men and notice Kahn and Berko giving the guard a piece of paper. I became aware of the situation and began to reevaluate my plan. A plan that's been set for months seems very distant. It looks like my "brothers" have turned their backs on me and told the guard about my plan. As I stand at my post with J, I feel very uneasy.

"J, I need to talk to you during break."

"Okay, something important?"

"Yeah, just a little bit."

"Well, we can talk now, you know?"

"No, it's okay. I prefer to wait." During break, I take J to the guard housing while everyone else is gone. "How long have you been here?"

"Twenty years."

"Do you ever want to leave?"

"I'd love to leave but I'm not sure where home is."

"Let's find home together and leave this place."

"Tumelo, you know we'll be gunned down for not paying our debt back."

"What debt? A debt that is agreed upon? A debt that is made by a false ruler, a ruler who owes many? You see this gun, J? I'm going to use it on you if you don't wake up and realize this isn't life. Gather some supplies and meet me in the woods before sunset. Don't ask any questions. Don't interact with anyone in the woods, be stealth, and I'll explain more later."

"I'm not the same, Melo. I'll shoot up this place. Okay, I agree. I'll gather supplies now and go stash them in a secure spot. Just watch the spot while I'm gone."

An hour goes by before he's back. Everything is in place. Guns, ammo, water, and some food. "We both know survival techniques, so we'll be fine if we run out. I was stopped by Ayo as well. He asked about my relationship with you and wanted to know why I was late to my post. I'm gonna need you to tell me what's going on here."

"J, I'll tell you but you have to stay silent."

"I'm already in this mess now, so go ahead and say what you've been keeping from me." After I finished telling him everything, he calmly shook his head and told me he would do the same thing in my situation. As the sky changes a different color, I inform J to go now. Leaving my post too early would alert everyone, so I stay a bit longer. I know with this eerie feeling something isn't right. I was going to kill Ayo in his bedroom, but there must be more to it. I'm going to kill him when the day comes. Before heading out, I pay off a slave to go shoot a gun in the bathroom to create a diversion. Once that shot goes off, I'm taking off to the woods. This will get the heat off me and clear up a path.

I hope Tumelo hurries up with the plan. Waiting here in the woods isn't the best especially with these wild animals. I need to take out Kahn and Berko before they greet Tumelo. Well, that's if they thought Tumelo would get that far after taking Ayo out. Beating their thought process is challenging yet empowering. My village got burned down because of Salem and his men. I'm surprised I never tried leaving before this moment. I hear crackling and laughter from the entrance of the woods. I notice two men with guns.

"If it weren't for Akin, we wouldn't be here, Berko. So selling out Tumelo will ensure our departure from hell. If he makes it past Ayo, which I would assume he doesn't, we'll greet him and blow his head off."

"No, I think we should torture him. I brought a knife. We should make him suffer like us."

"Interesting. Let's sit here and wait on him."

*Bang!* "I hope that shot was our plan and not to Tumelo." I creep up behind the two men. With their attention towards the village, they are unaware of what's going on behind them. I point both guns at them and add two more bangs! Down they go. I see Tumelo running to the woods.

"That's my boy! Our plan looks smooth thus far." Behind Tumelo, I see guards in the distance.

"J, let's go now!" We run away while they chase us. Lost inside the forest of Guinea, we still hear the men yelling behind us. We stop jogging and decide to make a plan.

"Tumelo, I've been with these guys for some years. They won't stop chasing until they find us. You know how to shoot and so do I. We have the advantage. Let's go on their outside. We'll be opposite from each other and fire down the middle. They'll drop, and if smart, they'll retreat. It's getting darker so we need to move fast and execute."

"Sounds good. Let's go." Opposite from J, I still see him from afar. We reach them as they come to a halt. I'm specifically looking for Ayo but trying to not be distracted and become selfish. J gives me the thumbs-up, then we unload fire at the opponent.

Bodies are dropping left and right. They aren't sure where the bullets are coming from. With all the commotion going on, I get a tap on my shoulder. I'm frozen, terrified to turn around. I drop my gun and plead. I get another tap, and I turn around slowly. Men with masks on and fired torches stand behind me. I'm speechless, scared, and back away slowly. Eventually, I end up in the middle of the battle. The warfare has stopped, and I notice we're all surrounded by these men. One of them uncovers his face and applauds. "I love what I just saw. A battle, two men take out a whole tribe. Well, almost, until we came. Which you should be lucky for. I'm sure the Europeans would love some warriors like you. Tonight you'll stay with us and be traded tomorrow morning. If someone would like to object, we can kill you in response. Any takers?"

"I'm not going anywhere. I don't know who you think you are to trade me off."

"Guards, take him out." I saw three guards take one of Ayo's men to the ground, and chop his head right off.

"Anybody else? That's what I thought. Now follow me."

Me and J connect and follow behind the guards. I notice there were only two men left from Ayo's warriors. Himself and another person. We arrived at their village and were placed in a pattern on the ground. "I know you all must be hungry. Tonight we'll eat legs, ribs, and whatever else you want." Moments later, the tribe brings out two deceased bodies. The guard who was killed and a young boy. Thrown in the fire, cut into pieces, the slicing begins. "There's no bad blood between you and us. As long as you four don't try to escape, we have no problems. But you must eat. This shows us respect." One by one, they give us each a piece of the body. I'm the youngest in the group, and all eyes are on me. I pick the leg meat off my plate and swallow without chewing. Disgusted and embarrassed, I looked down and began to tear up. "Tonight you'll sleep around the fire and be shipped off tomorrow morning. You men will be worth a fortune after I tell the Europeans about the battle."

*Chapter 7*

# Transition

"Wake up, they're here. Tumelo, just follow my lead. I've been to many of these trades, but never been auctioned off. Everything will be fine. Don't fight anyone. We're outnumbered and could get killed by anyone." We walk to the shore, and there it is. A brown boat just barely stopping before coming to an abrupt halt. Down comes a crew of White men. You can tell who the captain was based off the outfit, and he came with papers instead of chests like the others. Finally, our last stop before we set foot on confederate land.

"Hey, Captain. I have four battle-ready warriors that I found fighting in the forest. Pretty impressive skills. These men will go a long way in whatever field they are placed in."

"Thanks. Now take your reward and be gone. You four, today you become slaves of the American people and will obey every law. Follow me up the ship. You'll be placed with the other Black people here. Get ready for a long trip! But before we place you with the others, we have an area where you'll be stripped of clothing and your hair will be cut. You can keep your underwear on but everything else has to go."

After we finished going through the beginning process, a man who introduced himself as Christopher took us belowdecks. You can smell feces and see it lying around. Men lying in their vomit, cries from every section we pass—such an unsettling sight. The four of us were told to lie next to the slaves who were already there. I decided to lay near the back because there was no one to the left of me. This ship is definitely disease-filled. I hear coughs, sneezing, screams, and often, fights over space. Moments later, we were told to go up on deck to receive breakfast. Everyone rushed up to the deck like madmen. Rice and beans was an everyday meal according to some of the conversations I heard. Which is better than eating a human.

"Hey, Tumelo, I want you to know me and Ayo will kill you and J when the time is right. This isn't over, and you will feel our wrath."

"Did I just hear you threatening this boy? You know me and my crew don't condone in any bullying here. We lay down the rules and decide what happens to people. Do you understand me?"

"Christopher, this kid—"

"Shut up! I see you don't understand. Hey, everyone. Listen up. We have someone who wants to be an entertainer. Get your ass up there and dance in front of everyone." Seeing Ayo's guard get punished was amusing yet harsh. While dancing, he got beat with a whip, until he could no longer dance.

"J, did you see that?"

"Yes, I did. Just keep quiet and keep calm." This first day was my longest day. The second day was even worse. I saw a male crew member rape an enslaved male. I saw a speculum oris used to feed those who were sick of the everyday meals. They'd scream in pain while being forced to keep their mouth open. Terrified and full of pride, my mission was to kill Ayo and set out and find new land. Now that I've been taken away from my land, my plan has changed. I say my land like it was ever mine. A piece of earth that was owned by dictators and warlords. I've never had a place to call home. Maybe I'll find my brother someday, and we'll be able to have a place called home. Maybe not, but I know I'm destined for greatness as long as I have faith in myself.

Days got shorter, and weeks went by. Days were the same. Nights full of pain. Every day, lives were lost. People were beat, belittled, and dismantled. Men, women, and children were also raped. The sickness on the ship grew each day, both mentally and physically.

Disease-filled decks were a huge problem. Treated like sick animals, hundreds of slaves were thrown overboard in an attempt to stop the spread. This cleared up space among the ship. J and Ayo were still holding on to their lives. Ayo's guard got thrown over with the others. Although J was holding on to his life, I felt he was holding on to a secret. He developed a cough and was acting a bit strange. We became distant as he kept to himself. But eventually, he came out of his shell. "Tumelo, I want you to have my necklace. It was passed down to me from my father. Unfortunately, I was unable to have a child of my own, so I want to give this to you."

"What's going on, J?"

"I'm sick. I've been trying to keep it cool but I can't hold on any longer. Don't follow me on deck, but it's my time. I'd rather be with my creator than be with my destroyer. It's time I go. Our fallen brothers and sisters took the fall, now I'm ready to take the leap of faith. Goodbye, Tumelo."

As I walk up the steps to my final destination and enter outside, I alert the guards. It's pouring down rain. I guess that's a good thing, because it's hiding my tears. Guards start to walk behind me in a pursuit to get me to stay. Ignoring the comments, I look to the sky. Such a peaceful death. Eyes slowly close. Then I lean forward and fall into the afterlife.

*Splash!* That must've been J. This is a life that was lost too soon. One I'll never recover from. He did a lot for me. Forever grateful for him. Days later, we get notified we're close to the new colony. I'm not sure what it'll be like, but my new adventure begins in a new territory.

# Chapter 8

# Twist of Fate

"Welcome to the Confederate States of America. Remaining survivors, get up and exit the ship. Today you begin a life of hard labor and obedience. You'll be selected to your state of residence." As I look around, I'm surrounded by White people and different-looking Blacks. Blacks with a lighter complexion; Blacks that don't have that African look. Amused by what I saw, my thoughts began to wander. We're told to stand in line and wait for the auction to begin. As I look down the line, not many of us stand strong. Weakened by the food, forced to do unimaginable things to entertain the captain. Being belittled in every way definitely tears your pride down. Ayo is among those in the line. I think to myself that we're a product of our environment. According to stories back in Africa, Ayo was also captured by the former tribe leader, Salem. Ayo was someone looking for a way out but ended up ruling his own tribe. He, me, and others were taught to fight. We were taught that slavery was right. Could I blame him for all he's done? Some people can break the curse, but others stick to the system. Interrupted by a whip to my back, I scream out in pain.

"I said *boy*, several times. You better listen and get out your damn head. Be lucky I don't kill you. You're up next. Stand there and look decent so I can make my money, boy." White men examined me like a new invention. Soon enough, a slave owner from the state of Arkansas bought me out. Me and others, including Ayo, were forced to go on this "long journey."

No time was wasted. We were given clothes and food before leaving the slave port. "Okay, folks, we're going to start here in Virginia and work our way down to the southwest corner. You'll all be walking together until we reach the canal. I'm not sure where in Africa you people are from, nor do I care. But if you try us, it'll be your biggest mistake. Don't talk unless spoken to, and we'll be on good terms. Announce my name and the other horsemen by sir. Now that we're clear, let's begin our trip." After the White man spoke, we began our walk. Scared of what's to come, I just do what they say and walk. Even though my hatred for Ayo runs deep, I feel a little better that I'm not alone with all strangers. Foreign territory with a controlled environment—an environment that captures and trade people of my color. I'm not sure what's worse. This place feels like there's no escape. They've traveled a great distance to get us. In Africa, we were in war with each other. Tribal leaders had foreign mindsets which caused an imbalance between each other. Such an imbalance that greed led them to sell their own just to fight their own. Tears trickle down my cheek. What is life? Why am I here, alone? Nothing seems right. Maybe I should've jumped with J.

Hours go by, and my feet are blistering. They gave us random shoes that weren't the right sizes. We passed through towns that had other slaves in them. This slavery is a bit different. I saw people get whipped for no reason. Different-looking people; freedom looked a bit different. After going through a few towns, we came to a stop in the woods where we'd settle for the night. They chained us together to ensure no one would escape. We were given water and food to keep us energized for the next day. For the next two days, we repeated the process of traveling in the heat and encountering towns. By the time we reached the southwest corner of Virginia, my feet were numb and swollen. "Alright, from this point on, we'll separate you all into these two boats. This canal will lead us to the Mississippi River." They cramped us into two boats with little space for movement. Immediately, we were taught how to paddle. We were taught this because it was something we had to do for the remainder of our trip. We paddled vigorously through the water in fear of getting whipped for slowing down. We'd paddle through the day and find land to settle at for the night. There were times when there wasn't enough food or fresh water for anyone, which resulted in severe dehydration and hunger.

I wouldn't dare drink salt water, but some people became desperate. The White men drank their fresh water while we suffered. Lives were lost because of the intake of salt water and hunger. Their deaths led to more space and just enough resources to get through the day. According to the White men, we were a day away from our destination. I was nervous but frantic to get off this ship. The whip that slashed through my back left a mark that has gone untreated and became infected. I couldn't wait to get help, if that is a thing here. When we arrived in the Confederate States, men removed my necklace which had medical herbs on it. Each day, the heat would beat my back, and sweat would sting it. I could feel bugs flying on and off my back, eating the flesh. This last day, I was reminiscing on the past but wondering about the future. I have to keep in mind that I'll get through this even when I have doubt. "Alright, you slaves, I want you to find a place to stop on land for the night. We're not far from our destination, but it's getting dark and we need to be there early for branding." Not understanding what branding meant, we followed the orders and settled out for the night. Once I got some food in my system, I fell asleep quickly.

*Chapter 9*

# Lost and Found

Wake up! Today is the day you meet your master. Round up and get on the boat. With no energy to spare, I get up and head to the boat. Slowly gathering myself together, I get pushed to the ground. "Tumelo, don't think I forgot about you. Once I get you alone you'll be like the rest of the worthless Africans. You'll be dead. That's a promise, not a threat." Lucky for Ayo, no one in authority saw it. We all enter the boats and make our way to Arkansas. The White men weren't joking. This place wasn't far at all. We got there super early and took a brief walk to the site. After we got off the boat, another set of slaves entered.

"Before releasing you to housing, you must be branded to show your property of information. Follow me. This is where that'll happen." He showed us the venue, and I was set to go first. I entered, and I instantly felt the hot air. My back began to sting.

"Hey, boy, get over here." He grabbed this iron stick and looked for a place to put it on my skin. "I think I'm going to put this on your back." When he put it on my skin, I screamed in pain, then passed out.

My eyes slowly begin to open. It seems that I'm in a cabin. I don't remember walking here. "Hey, sleepy, are you feeling any better? You've slept the day away. You passed out and I noticed some marks on your back. I've treated you and I promise you'll feel a lot better. Tonight there's a meeting for the new slaves that'll go over housing and everything that you need to know. You'll be staying here tonight for recovery. The meeting begins in two hours. If you're hungry, you may go out and get something to eat. I'll direct you."

"Thank you very much. Yes, please direct me to the food."

"I knew you were hungry. Come over here. Before I release you, what's your name, so I can put it in our documents."

"My name is Tumelo. And yours?"

"That's interesting. Me and my husband were going to name my son that. That's before these White folks forced us to use American names. His name is Melvin, and my name is Mabel. Let's get you some food now. Go out the door and go past the big white house and you'll see the food on your right-hand side. There will be people in that area, which you'll see gathering around." Once I walked out of the medical shack, I felt a strong presence of hatred. People were looking at me as if I disgusted them. These people weren't White nor were they Black. As I continued walking, I eventually saw my people of color. There were tables with bowls of food so you could serve yourself. The other people sat in another area with their own tables.

I made my food and sat alone. I didn't want to be bothered. But of course, that didn't last long. This male sat right across from me and asked how I was doing. I ignored him hoping he'd leave. "Just not going to respond, huh? Well, I'll tell you about myself. I'm from Africa. My parents died and I left a little baby brother whom I've never talked to. My dad died because I made a foolish decision to run away from a tribe that tried to enslave us. My mother died for me. It was I who was supposed to be punished for something I didn't do. Her head chopped off right in front of me. I didn't want to leave my brother but I was traded after this incident."

I stopped eating. That sounds similar to my story. I look at him for a clearer picture this time, and he has a patch over his left eye. My heart began beating fast, and tears began to fill my eyes. "Sir, could you please take off your patch?

"Don't call me sir. I don't own you. Call me brother. That's what the rest of the Africans call each other. My former tribal leader slashed my eye and it left a huge mark." At this point, the tears are trickling down my face. "Why're you crying?"

"Because my name is Tumelo, and you're my brother... Akin." Before the slave orientation kicked off, me and my brother spent time talking about the past and the future. I haven't smiled or felt so good inside. We hugged and cried for a while. "Which unit are you in?"

"I haven't been checked into housing because of my injuries. I've been staying at the medical shack to recover from a slash on my back."

"Speaking of getting beat, thank you for telling me Ayo is here. I want you to go to that meeting tonight, and don't get in any trouble. Ayo won't be attending it due to injuries. I thought I passed him earlier but now I know that was indeed him."

# Chapter 10

# Past and Present

"Alright, brother. Go ahead. I'm going to see you tomorrow at breakfast. I'm going to find Ayo before the meeting starts. Have a good night." Years of pain caused by one person. Tonight's the night I torture him. I search for a few minutes before I spot him.

"Hey, Ayo, come with me. I'm a guard here. I have a position of authority for you since you're an older guy. Let's step into the medical shack for a moment."

"No problem. How do you know my name?"

"The slave master mentioned it earlier."

"Speaking of him, do I need to attend the orientation soon?"

"Nope, there's no need for it. Find yourself a seat and relax. I have to go to the back. Hey, Mabel, do you remember Ayo?"

"Yes, how could I forget?"

"Well, I got him waiting in the front. I'm going to torture him. Give me your supplies and a rope. I'll be back."

"No way. He's here?"

"Yep, and so is Tumelo. Right now let's focus on Ayo. Hey, Ayo, come on back here, brother. We have to evaluate you before we can give you this position. Lay in bed. Mabel here will strap you down for testing."

"What testing?"

"It's a general diagnostic to make sure you are certified to do the following position. I'll be right back. Lay tight."

"Okay, Mr. Ayo. Let me strap you in."

"Nurse, how about I strap you in? You look just like this woman I used to take care of."

"Oh, does she?"

"Yes, she does. Back already?"

"Let me take this patch off. Maybe I remind you of someone as well."

Akin…it's been forever."

"I know. Good thing we'll be spending the next few days together."

"What do you mean?"

"Don't worry. I'm going to place this rope over your mouth and show you how much I missed you."

"Akin, please don't hurt me. I'm sor—"

"On the first night, we'll start with your toes." One at a time, I sliced each toe off. He tried screaming in pain. But he didn't stand a chance against the rope. Once he passed out from the pain, me and Mabel headed out. Tomorrow will be even better.

The sun crept up slowly as the morning introduced itself again. Still amazed by that meeting last night, I'm in shock about a lot. Specifically the Civil War. We could be free men by joining, but where does that place us slaves? Say we win; will we be treated differently? Given land? That sounds a bit far-fetched considering the Indians got theirs taken. Another shock was me thinking our owner would be White, not a Native American. I guess that's a way to say sorry for taking over their land; make them feel like they have control whilst controlling them. I don't feel like any of them like us Black people but must accept us for the hard labor. We're quite the same, paid off to do what they want. Africans paid in guns, money, and other wants. Indians paid off just to give them a sliver of land that has *I'm not sorry* written all over it. Native Americans own each other just like we do. The only difference is they fought and were lied to. Some of their tribes came together and still lost the battle with these White men. Disgusting as it sounds, we gave in and sold each other for greed. To them, we're just another race on their land. We don't want to be here. Well, I don't. I wanted change between the African communities, but the turmoil is too strong. It's too strong in Africa. But what if it's not too strong here? What if we came together and stood up? What if this is a start to something new, a partnership that could put us in front of the line?

While getting ready to leave the medical room from my overnight stay, I noticed a trace of blood on one of the beds. I didn't notice this once I came back last night. The room was really dark. A sheet was covered over this person, and I had no choice but to look. As I uncovered it, I noticed it was Ayo. His toes were cut off, and I instantly knew who did it. He was dead asleep, but this was an opportunity to add to the pain. I grabbed some nearby scissors, lifted the rope, and got a tight grip on his tongue. Snap! His tongue was nonexistent, and he felt every bit of it. I put the rope and sheet back on and left right away. As I walk to breakfast, I notice the Indians. Instead of giving them a cold stare, I smile as an act of change. That morning, I met with Akin to discuss what happened at the meeting and to talk about life in general. I discussed the potential of connecting with the Indians, and he looked at me sideways. To him, this is life, but I had to remind him of our story. We didn't come this far to only come this far. For the next few days, we worked in the field picking cotton. We had other duties such as cooking and making sure we maintained proper guidelines of slavery here.

# Chapter 11

# Our Land

A few days is all it took for me to realize that something needs to happen. A change needs to occur. On the fourth day, I gathered the Black people during breakfast, lunch, and dinner to discuss a need to leave. Of course, Akin joined in and eventually led the group. On the fifth day, I decided to make friends on the other side. But again, we're on the same side. I was looked down on for trying to make a connection, even told to leave their group by elder Indians. The master warned me this could lead to homicide amongst the two groups. Some wanted to make that connection with me. The most trouble I had was getting the Black people who were born into slavery onboard. They were content on being fed every day and working twelve-hour days. Comfortable with not knowing anyone but themselves. Comfortable with the master taking their wives and creating children. Comfortable with not wanting change. But tomorrow's a new day. A change.

This morning, I woke up with an attitude. We may feel the same as a group, but no one is ready to make that jump across. I head to breakfast, giving the Indians another smile and wave. It's only been a few days, but the more I do this act of kindness, the more I receive it back. I get to my group of people and ask them, "How many of you are wanting change?" Most people respond with yes. Others are silent. "For those of you who want change, what have you done to fix our situation? Don't answer that question, I'll answer it for you. The answer is nothing. I know all of you had the history lesson during your first time here. Did it not occur to anyone that we have similar stories? Similar build?" Three Indian guards walk up and tell me it's time to get to work. "Yes, it's time to work together."

"What?"

"You heard me. I'm not working in a field. I'm not working for someone who's in the same position I am."

"I'm going to whip you if you don't stand down."

"The only thing I do is stand up, and so should you three." All the commotion got the attention of the other Indians. When they arrived, every Black person stood up and was prepared for a show-down. Even the satisfied ones who didn't want change.

"No, neither side will fight. This is the closest we've stood together when not working in the field. I don't care if you beat me, but today this ends here. I'll die before I work another second for you. It's easy to fight the people who are just like you. Under American control and fighting for nothing. I'm not sure what the Confederates told you, but you must be gullible. Your land is gone. Don't think that they'll give it back. They're fighting against each other, which will unite the two lands but will have one ruling. One ruling, one nation, but two attitudes. The only thing that you can't read is a mind, but you can see the skin tone. Me and my people are Black. We were traded to a foreign area. I'm uncomfortable being here. I'm hated by you and the Whites. I feel the tension. So if you're going to beat me, do it. I'm not sure how that'll go over with my people, but I suggest you rethink your actions. And for us Black people, hostility among the same group of people is uncalled for. We never took the chance to get to know them, comfortable in your own skin. Comfortable on a stolen land that you got traded to. Comfortable with not fighting back. We lost the war with ourselves. That's why we're here, tension between provinces. Greed, wanting to own it all and kill anyone who wanted a piece. Selfish! We lost the battle! Indians, you lost the battle as well! Tribal warfare according to orientation. So selfish, so dark, so cold-hearted. The master here captured you along with White men. Promoted violence within tribes, to kill you off easier.

"The thing that I noticed is that not all of you Indians talk together. Which tells me that you are from different tribes. But in this moment, you stand as one. I'm asking both groups today, to be one. Let's be one. The North and South are fighting. I say we join in. We join in because we didn't when it was time. We didn't join in with our respective countries to avoid futuristic problems. We'll be the ones to tell the story, the ones who tried to make it right. If we succeed, the country is simply ours. If we don't, let's pray for the future. Before we plan this out, I must know who's in?"

"I'm in." The master appeared from behind the crowd. "I heard everything you said, and I'm in." Both crowds including the master are crying. The Black people and Indians soon united. Crying of emotions and pain that we've all been through. For the rest of the day, we sat around and enjoyed each other's company and began to learn more about one another. Most importantly, that night, our lives were about to change. Each group chose their leader as we were about to embark on a journey of our own. The master was chosen by the Indians, and we chose Akin as ours. As the time narrowed down, it was time to plan. Akin and the master would lead us in a speech.

"Attention, everyone. For those of you who didn't hear my name earlier, my name is Akin. The speech my younger brother gave to all of us meant a lot and we need to take action. From now on, we're all brothers and must fight together. Not all of you are going to go. Some must stay here and watch the camp. We will return once victory is ours. This country will be ours and filled with our people. We will unite and be successful."

# Chapter 12

# New Ties

"Tonight will be the first night of many more to come with us being together. Tonight we'll also leave in search of finding more people like us to go against the Confederates and anyone who stands in our way. I'll step down and let the master take over."

"Before I begin my speech, I'd like everyone to call me Elu. I'm not a master; I'm a trader. Someone who wants to make right of his wrongdoings. I captured and I traded people to the Confederates to keep them off me. I'm a disgrace but not for long. This is our land. We know this territory. We'll face people that won't join us that'll look like us. In order to not leave a trace, we must kill villages. We will face Confederates that will not like the sight of equality. We must take them down. For those of you who are not okay with killing or too weak, you'll stay here and protect families from dying and any invasion. Pack up, hug your families tight because tonight we leave. We'll meet at the white house and go on from there in an hour. Tumelo, I'll meet you there."

"I have to say my goodbyes to Mabel and Melvin."

"Okay. I'll see you then."

By the time I reached my family, the word was out, and my wife knew what was next. I kissed both of them on the cheek and gave them hugs. I held the tears back. My heart was broken. It broke in

through. We tried to stay calm until nighttime hit, but it was hard. As we sat around for hours, we saw the Black man get beat for fun. We saw children with bandages, and women taken away from their husbands. Finally, it was nighttime, and it was time to get Elu and other brothers. Akin is much bigger than me, so he went to go help out Elu along with a few others. Me and the other people went to get our brother and sisters.

"Be careful, Tumelo. Scream if needed. Meet us back where we waited."

"Okay, brother." Then we split. Before me and the others entered the house where Elu is locked down, we went to the guard's station. The guard was asleep upon arrival, but that didn't stop us from slicing his head right off. After that occurred, we made our way to the house. I stood at the front while I sent the others to the back door. The front door was locked, but the back door wasn't. As I looked in the side window, my brothers helped me get inside. Two people each stayed at the front and back doors, while me and another person went upstairs. Three doors stood in front of us as we opened each quietly. The first door had a woman and what appeared to be a guard next to her. I sent my brother into the room as he took care of business. The second door I opened contained Elu. He was strapped to the bed and was frantically trying to get out. I began cutting to set him free. His eye was black, and he had been beat up pretty good. As I finished unraveling the straps, a voice appeared from behind me.

"You thought I didn't know he had others with him, huh?" *Bang!* My heart dropped, knees buckled, and I was unable to move. I thought that bullet was coming to me. I turned around and saw the master's body drop, with my brother standing on top of him with a gun.

"I guess grabbing this came in handy."

"Thank you. You saved my life." I finished getting Elu out of the straps, then hugged my Indian brother. We left the house and went outside where Tumelo and a new crew awaited our return. We all hugged one another as we knew we'd be on this journey together.

*Chapter 13*

# Feds

For weeks, we fought together, building a reputation in Arkansas. We found more people who wanted to be a part of our group, and others who didn't. We saw plantations run by the White men with Blacks and Indians as slaves. We saw nice slave owners who didn't want any trouble. We could see the good in the evil but didn't allow that to overcome what we wanted. The night before we reached Oklahoma, we all lay there and told stories around multiple fires. "Hey, guys, before we cross over tomorrow, I want to let you know that I love you all. We're sacrificing a lot by fighting for what's rightfully ours. Like I've mentioned before, we're going to seek help from the other tribes. This isn't Confederate or Union land. It's strictly Indians. Let's use words rather than weapons. We don't want to kill these guys, but we'll defend at any cost." After Elu's speech, we all got comfortable and went to sleep.

*Bang! Bang!* "Mother, please wake up. I hear gunshots. Mother wake up, get up now."

"Melvin, what's going on, honey?"

"I heard gunshots and voices outside, Mom."

"I'm sure it's nothing, baby. You were probably dreaming." *Bang!* I quickly grab my son and put him into a wooden closet. I look outside, and I see horses and torches. I look a bit closer and it's men wearing gray coats, going to shack after shack. Screams started to pour out as everyone became aware of the situation. Ambushed, we were on the losing side. The soldiers spread out over the place, daring a single person to come out and defend. The bullets got louder as the soldiers came closer and closer. Eventually, it was the medical shack's turn. I run to my son and tell him I love him and to not leave until he no longer hears voices and gunshots. I slam the door and wait until they reach the back room. I hear all the injured patients screaming in the room until they're hit with a bullet. The door to the back room opens, and I wait for him to enter. With scissors in my hand, I'm ready to strike. The moment I see the side of his face, I stab him right in the head, causing him to bleed out. After that, two soldiers came into the room and pinned me down.

With a slight crack in the closet, I saw my mother struggle. I saw her fight for survival, and eventually, I heard her last breath before she was shot. She lay there motionless as the soldiers left the shack. I stayed as quiet as I could. Tears ran sprints down my face. I asked myself why us. Why is this life? Why must this happen? What did we do? I questioned everything until I drifted off asleep.

"Good morning, fellas. Let's eat, then saddle up. Today's that day."

"Akin, I'm not sure why but I have a strange feeling. I don't know what it is but my stomach is turning."

"Tumelo, if you need anything, let me know. I'm here for you."

"Akin, do you think Mabel and Melvin will be there once we return?" Tears ran down his face when I asked him this, and he replied with no, but he's hopeful. After we left the site, we crossed into Indian territory after a couple of hours. No sign of anything yet. We traveled in a different direction, headed towards the north. Which led to our first meeting with a huge group of Indians. We all walked together with high hopes of forming an alliance. As we got closer, we noticed we were having a meeting with us. They all wore gray coats as if that were mandatory. I began to hear whispers among our people. On high alert, they began walking towards us. A few moments later, we came face-to-face with them. "Why're you on our land? Which tribe do you belong to?"

"Elu says we don't belong to any tribe. We're a brotherhood. We're a family."

"You can't be family with people who don't look like you."

"Yes, you can. Give us a few moments to explain what we're about. I see you have Black people on your land? Why're they here?"

"We own them. We teach them how to fight and live life the Confederate way."

"Confederates? This is Indian land but you've decided to side with them? We may not know each other and come from different tribes, but in your heart, you know this isn't right."

"It is right. If you can't beat them, join them. This way we won't have to fight the White men and will be able to have our land forever. We'll help them out and they'll keep their word. We'll also make a treaty with other tribes to have peace in our state. If anyone tries to stop us or them, they're considered enemies."

"By the looks of the people you have standing here, it seems you've been capturing people and building an army. You've raided slave plants and got people to side with you. Which means fewer people to defend against the Union."

"You've disrespected all of us. Now we must kill you."

"We don't wish to fight you."

"You have no choice. Boys, attack." A fight broke out between our two groups. It was pretty cool to see my brothers in action, but at the same time this is what we tried to prevent. We're fighting and killing us. As the fight went on, they gained the advantage because they had more men. Black men and Indians joined the battle, and we began to retreat. We scattered as they were able to have ample ammunition. We ran, and they gave chase. Many people in our group dropped like flies due to the bullets hitting them from behind. Me and Akin stayed near each other the whole way. Dodging bullets and trees as we scrambled away. We ran for a long time and ended up in the town of Pea Ridge, Arkansas. With the Confederates still on our trail, we ran into a new danger. A sight that terrified me. White confederates with their gray coats walking our way. "Hey, Tumelo, I want you to know that I love you. No matter what happens, I love you. When I got shipped off, I thought about you every day. I'm happy to see the man you turned into. I'm not sure what's about to happen right now but it doesn't look good. Before anything happens, I want to give you this necklace. This resembles us. You've been my motivation since day one."

*Chapter 14*

# Cursed

"If one of us has to die, it'll be me. I created this for us. I ran out the house. I let my emotions get the best of me and left you behind. You're great and you have more life to live. We all do, but we all die at some point. Everybody dies but not everyone lives. This seems like our final destination, or mine."

"Akin, I'm not leaving your side. I'm tired of running. We're in this together."

As we talk, the Confederates close in on us. "What're you two doing out here in the open?"

As we began to talk, the Indians from Oklahoma appeared and surrounded us. "These two are trying to ruin our army. They've been capturing slaves and building their own team to defeat us Confederates."

"If this is true, where's their army? They look like runaway slaves, and everybody knows how we deal with them."

"Sir, take my life. This was my idea and he had nothing to do with it."

"I'm happy you know the consequences of the actions you presented. Both of you will die. Close your eyes as you enter the sky."

"The Union is here! The Union is here!"

"On second thought, how about you help us win this battle and you won't suffer." They threw us guns and expected us to battle. Me and Akin looked at each other and agreed.

Bullets rang out from all corners. This attack looked planned by the Union troops. As I held the gun up, Akin tugged on me and said, "We're not doing this. Let's back away and find a way out." Eventually finding our way out of all the madness, soldiers were too distracted to realize we weren't in line with them anymore. We hugged each other tight and promised to never leave one another. *Bang!* His grip loosened, and he fell to the ground. He was shot from behind by the Indian Confederate leader from Oklahoma.

"You didn't think you guys were getting away, right?" I cried out loud, a war cry as he was slowly dying. I lay on top of him, begging for Akin to not die on me. "Your next up, little guy. It's time for you to go as well. Join your brother. That's exactly what he'd want."

I get up and walk away slowly, begging him not to shoot. I didn't want to pull my gun out. I was stuck. Waiting for a bullet to end my life. As he points the gun at me, he grins a grin full of evil. A grin of forgotten worth, a grin of greed. *Bang!* He drops the gun and falls down. Looking past him, I see that my brother used the gun that was given to him to take out my attacker. He saved my life. His gun fell to the ground, and his eyes were closing. He was dead. I ran away, not knowing where to go. I was lost. Lost mentally, I tried everything. I've lost everything, I tried to rewrite history and came up short. I traveled for days towards what I thought was the right direction. Without food and water, my body began to break down. I passed through towns we completely cleared out in hopes of finding fresh food and water. I began to give up. The more I walked, the more my body felt weak. Eventually, I could no longer hold up. I was always big on challenges being mental, and this was a battle of both. I had no more tears to shed and my body was unable to cooperate. I never thought I'd do the impossible, but I pulled out the gun from the battle and looked at it. This could be the solution to no more pain. A quick easy death. No more beatings. No more failed attempts of a better life. I'll always have to understand that this will always be the position of a Black man. We turned on each other and aren't liked by anyone. There's good people, but not enough good can outdo the bad. The cons outweigh the pros. I aimed the gun at my head and pulled the trigger.

*Bang!* I hide quickly. I don't want to see the bad people again. I waited there for hours until I came out again. It was a foggy day, and I couldn't see much outside. I've been traumatized. I've been in a town full of dead people. My mother's body still lay in the same position as the others here. A town full of dead people. I must go now. I need to find my dad and Tumelo. Hopefully, there's someone that knows where they are. I gather water and food, then start to leave town. With the fog being so heavy, I couldn't see anything. As I walked towards the border of the town, I stepped and what appeared to be liquid. As I looked down, I noticed it was blood. Warm blood, which seemed a bit weird. I walked a little more, and my feet hit an object. It was a body. Brains splattered everywhere, I began to search the body for anything that could help along the way. I discovered a necklace. A necklace that my father wore. Why was it not on him? Did he die? Did he leave us stranded? Then I realized this was my uncle Tumelo. My thoughts were racing. No kid should go through this. As I sobbed, an image appeared from the fog. A woman reached out to me. "Little boy, let me help you." Not knowing if I should follow her, she grabbed my hand and we disappeared into the fog.

# *About the Author*

Jermaine Monteil Huddleston is currently a business owner of both DominantXV and Maine Publishing. Along with being a business owner, he also plays rugby in Glendale, Colorado. Pursuing his degree in business administration, his real passion is writing. With this being his first book to the public, look for him to make many more enticing books. This twenty-three-year-old author is destined for greatness as he's determined to deliver the best content to empower your mind. Embark on this journey with him and find yourself wanting more and more!